If Your Price Is Right

A *"Holy Rock Chronicles"* Short

Shelia Writes Books

Perfect Stories About Imperfect People Like You...and Me!

SCANLIFE

Get more Info About Shelia E. Bell books!

MULTI-AWARD WINNING NATIONAL BESTSELLING AUTHOR

SHELIA E. BELL

ISBN: 979-8-9867834-0-6

Library of Congress Control Number: 2023906526

www.sheliawritebooks.com
Aurora, Colorado

If Your Price Is Right

A "Holy Rock Chronicles" Short

Shelia Writes Books

Perfect Stories About Imperfect People Like You...and Me!

SCANLIFE

Get more Info About Shelia E. Bell books!

"Perfect Stories About Imperfect People Like You...and Me"

"Holy Rock Chronicles Shorts"

"Holy Rock Chronicles" is a captivating spinoff series of short stories that take you on a journey into the intriguing lives of the notorious members of the Graham and McCoy families from the national bestselling "My Son's Wife" series. These shorts are specially crafted to provide an exclusive, behind-the-scenes look at the characters' lives while I continue to pen the next thrilling installment in this captivating family saga. I am grateful for your continued support and for choosing to read my work. Thank you!

<u>Books 4- 6</u>
(Best if Read after Book 12 - Redeeming Holy Rock)

Christian Black, Esq. (4)
If Your Price is Right (5)
Love Shoulda Brought You Home (6)

one

"To exact revenge for yourself or your friends is not only a right, it's an absolute duty." S. Larsson

Trevor Price strode into the bustling Italian restaurant and picked up his dinner, something he often did whenever his fiancé, Niesha, a traveling nurse, was out of state on assignment.

Tonight, Trevor had chosen this particular restaurant because he could get one of his favorites, chicken saltimbocca.

The aroma of the prosciutto and butter garlic sauce filled the car, making his belly growl. As he savored the aroma, he felt a flutter of excitement in his stomach. After a long day in the office and attending court, he was looking forward to enjoying a quiet evening in his upscale condo in Covington, Tennessee.

Upon entering his tastefully furnished abode, he eagerly shed the constraints of his tailored suit and indulged in a rejuvenating shower. While showering, his mind wandered to Niesha. The thought of her ignited a fiery passion within him, and he couldn't help but marvel at his good fortune.

Niesha was a treasure - she was cute, confident, smart, a little sassy, and a thrill-seeker at heart. All the things he liked in a woman.

After his shower, he sat at his kitchen island and enjoyed every delectable bite of his food while scrolling on his iPhone. He shook his head when he ran across a woman on social media acting like a first class 'Karen' shouting at a terrified grandmotherly-looking woman for not putting her shopping cart in the holding stall. For some reason, the irate "Karen" made him think of his client's ex-wife, Rianna McCoy, and the less-than-pleasant exchanges they had during her and Hezekiah's divorce. He hadn't seen or heard from her until last Sunday when she suddenly appeared outside New Holy Rock.

Trevor often attended church when Niesha was out of town. She had no interest in attending religious services.

On this particular Sunday, Rianna, with Tiny, her bold companion, popped in front of his BMW, forcing him to come to a screeching halt.

"Wait! I need to talk to you," Rianna declared with urgency.

2

Trevor was taken aback by the dangerous situation. "Are you out of your mind?" he exclaimed as he recognized Rianna as the fool who had jumped in front of his car. Had she followed him to the church or had he simply missed her in church service?

"I need to talk to you. It's important, very important," Rianna insisted.

Tiny, with her butt-length purple braids swaying from side to side, stood next to Rianna, keeping a watchful eye as if she were poised to protect her friend.

Trevor was stunned to silence. He couldn't believe Rianna McCoy and her friend had almost caused him to run them down.

He tried to shoo them away. "Look, there's nothing for us to talk about. My client doesn't owe you another red cent. Now, please, get out of my way," he snapped, his eyes darting around the church parking lot for any signs of a security guard.

Rianna was resolute as she closed in on Trevor's car. "I know you're Hezekiah's Power of Attorney. Stiles told me to come to you," she declared, undeterred by Trevor's growing frustration.

Trevor ground his teeth. "I don't have time for this foolishness. If you want to talk, call my office and make an appointment," he snarled, "like any normal person."

"Don't you dare talk to me like that," she yelled as if he was cussing her out.

Despite Tiny's pleas for Rianna to move aside, Rianna held her ground, locking eyes with Trevor.

Finally, with a shrug, she stepped back, allowing Trevor to drive off, his car cutting through the church lot with a swerve.

Driving away, Trevor breathed a sigh of relief, but he knew this was far from over. From his personal experience, he knew Rianna's fire was not easily quenched, and her determination was a force to be reckoned with.

two

"Let pressure pass over and through you. That way you can't be harmed by it." Brian Herbert

Two weeks after their rowdy parking lot encounter, Rianna was seated in the outer area of Trevor's office.

The luxurious lifestyle she had been growing accustomed to as Hezekiah's wife and First Lady had been cruelly ripped away in the divorce, but she was determined to do something about it, starting with this meeting with Trevor Price.

"Ms. McCoy, if you would follow me," Miss Jones interjected, her tone crisp and urgent.

"Come on, Tiny."

"Nah, I'm going to go wait in the car. I need to call my baby daddy back and cuss him out. He just text me talkin' bout he gon' take my son out of town with him and some new heffa he met. I don't think so," Tiny said, throwing her braids back off her face.

"*Whaat?* No, he didn't, girl."

"Oh, yes he did," Tiny shot back. "He got me messed up!"

Miss Jones, crossing her arms, stood to the side, listening to the two women go back and forth.

"The nerve of him. I'm tellin' you, Tiny, these men are working my last nerves," Rianna replied, her voice steely.

"Well, he got the wrong one, baby. I'm not going for the okie-doke," said Tiny.

"Look, I gotta go, so you go on back to the car. I'll be out as soon as this is over. It shouldn't take long to get what I came here for."

Rianna gave Miss Jones a side eye and proceeded to follow her up the hall. They stopped in front of a door with the name ATTORNEY TREVOR E. PRICE etched into it.

"Please, take a seat," Trevor invited as she entered his office.

Rianna sat across from Trevor, her eyes blazing with anger.

"What can I help you with, Miss McCoy?"

"Don't play me. You know darn well what I'm here for. I need money. Hezekiah left me high and dry and I'm not standing for it. I don't care if we're divorced or not, he needs to do right by me. With your help, Hezekiah has taken everything from me. He cut off my credit cards, took my position as Minister of Music away from me, and basically banned me from New Holy Rock."

"All of that was addressed and settled in the divorce," Trevor explained as he studied the attractive but loony ex-wife of Hezekiah.

"I don't wanna hear nothing about what was settled in the divorce. I'm telling you, you need to do something. Did you see me limping in here? I'm still injured and it's all because of him."

"You were compensated for that already. My client's insurance paid your doctor bills and you were also awarded a monetary settlement."

"Settlement?" Rianna pouted. "Are you serious? That was kibbles and bits, and you know it. Plus, I would never be in this position if it wasn't for him. He's nothing but a liar and a good-for-nothing, lowdown, dirty dog. And if you don't help me, you're no better than him," she carried on.

"I'm not sure what you think I can do for you," Trevor repeated, his voice calm.

Rianna wasn't listening. "You're his power of attorney. I need money and you can make it happen. I can barely afford to buy food or pay my rent. I was let go from my job and I had to file for disability. I have nothing left," she spat, her voice trembling with anger.

"I'm sorry to hear that, but like I said, I can't help you. You received everything you were entitled to in the divorce," Trevor repeated, shaking his head and raising his palms in a gesture of helplessness. "There's nothing else I can do. Now, if you'll excuse me, I think we're done." Trevor pushed back from his desk and rose to his feet.

"Hol' up. You're going to get me some more money." Rianna was not ready to give up. "Don't act like you're Mr. Goody Two-Shoes. I know things about you. Your reputation is far from clean."

Trevor's irritation grew with each word Rianna spoke. "I don't have time for your games, Mrs. Jamison," he sneered, referring to her by her maiden name in an attempt to intimidate her, "or your threats."

Rianna rose to her feet, grabbing hold of the arm of the chair to sturdy herself. With a slight limp, she walked around the desk to confront Trevor.

"You can be sure this is no game. I know you're a cheat and a scammer. You hide behind that law degree while you rob people of their hard-earned money."

Trevor remained unfazed. "This meeting is over. Leave, and don't ever come here threatening me again," he said with eerie calmness.

He walked past Rianna to the door, holding it open for her to leave.

Rianna rolled her eyes as she stormed past him. "This isn't over," she muttered under her breath. "You can count on that."

three

"The harder you work for something, the greater you'll feel when you achieve it." Success.com

Trevor scanned through unread emails, checked his weekly calendar, and then stood to leave his office for the day.

"Ms. Jones, I'm shutting it down." He slightly yawned and quickly covered his mouth.

Ms. Jones looked up from her computer, smiled, and replied with her usual evening pleasantries. "I'll see you tomorrow. Have a nice evening."

"You too," Trevor replied. "It's been a draining day, to say the least."

"Yes, it sure has. Especially after that meeting with Rianna McCoy."

Trevor's face darkened. "You got that right. I tell you, that woman is pure evil." His hand balled into a fist, unconsciously.

Ms. Jones raised an eyebrow, "That's a rather strong description, don't you think? Especially coming from you."

"Maybe," Trevor growled, "but I call it like I see it. All I can say is Hezekiah McCoy better be glad he divorced her."

Ms. Jones threw up her hands. "I'm sure he is. Now, you go on home. We'll talk tomorrow." She giggled but then stopped when she saw his serious expression.

"I suggest you not stay much longer either. We have another busy day tomorrow."

"I know," Ms. Jones replied, "I'm not far behind you. Oh, before you leave, remember your phone meeting with Xavier McCoy is tomorrow morning at nine and you have a video call with your client, Samson Asbury, at ten-thirty."

Trevor stopped in his tracks and looked at Ms. Jones. "Thanks, I'll look over Asbury's file tonight, but I'm prepared."

As Trevor confidently strode down the hall, a sense of pride washed over him. At thirty-three, he was already a successful attorney, known for his expertise in divorce and tort cases.

He inherited his mother's Italian features and curly black hair, and his father's devilishly handsome African-American looks.

Growing up and even now, Trevor was the envy of many, with his olive skin being the perfect mixture of his mother's pale complexion and his father's deep melanin skin tone.

Trevor's heart was irreparably shattered at age twelve. That's when his mother abandoned him and his father, leaving them to cope with the harsh aftermath of her departure. Despite his father's fervent pleas to God for her to return, she never came back.

From what he recalled seeing as a kid, his parents were always kissing and hugging each other, or laughing about something. He didn't remember hearing or seeing them argue. Maybe that was the problem. Maybe things were too perfect. As a grown man, he could very well see now how that could have been the case. Nothing is supposed to be perfect in life.

Years after she left them, when Trevor was fifteen, he and his father sadly discovered his mother had begun her life anew with a whole other family in Italy. The pain and heartbreak caused by her abandonment lingered, a constant wound that refused to heal. She had moved on with her life, a life Trevor and his father were not part of. The painful realization struck him deeply, but as time passed, an emotional scab formed, concealing the wound she had inflicted upon his heart.

Trevor regretted how much he'd put his father through when he was a hard-headed, wild, and unruly teenager. Yet, he remained focused when it came to his schoolwork. He thrived on learning, making his father proud in that instance.

His father inspired him to attend Harvard and follow in his footsteps. The man was a great example of what a man, a real father, a daddy, looked like. He succumbed to prostate cancer days shy of Trevor receiving his juris doctorate.

As he stepped into the elevator, Trevor shook his head to clear his mind from the onslaught of thoughts. He had other things more important than dwelling on matters of his past. He'd trained himself not to let his personal life interfere with his rising success. He took a deep breath. He had much to be thankful for. He reminded himself of the strong, determined person he had become.

four

"Money can't buy friends, but you can get a better class of enemy." Spike Milligan

Trevor and Xavier McCoy had struck up an unlikely friendship after Xavier's ex-partner, Ian Hodges, introduced Xavier to handle his divorce. When the divorce was called off, Xavier and Trevor continued to talk and hang out on occasion.

"Bruh, I had to call and tell you about your ex-stepmother. That woman is looney tunes!" Trevor bellowed over videochat.

Xavier laughed. "What's going on? What's she done now?" He leaned forward in his office chair. His eyes narrowed in suspicion as he briefly gazed from the screen and out the window at the gathering storm.

"Man, she almost caused a car crash Sunday before last when I was trying to leave

New Holy Rock," Trevor cried, his arms flailing in frustration.

"Are you serious? Yep, that woman is insane. And please, don't call her my stepmother. I barely have a relationship with my father, so you can imagine how I feel about his choice of wife," Xavier spat, his eyes rolling in disgust.

Trevor let out a harsh laugh.

"She may have been a good minister of music, but when it comes to normal human behavior, she's in a league of her own, completely unhinged," Xavier added.

"Yeah, I'm starting to understand what you mean. She's a real piece of work," Trevor nodded in agreement. "What about calling her the step monster?" He chuckled darkly.

"Nah, why don't we *not* call her my *step* anything? What did she want?"

"Money, what else." Trevor sneered, his voice heavy with sarcasm.

"Money? She's lost it," Xavier said, his head shaking in disbelief. "You and I both know Pops treated her fairly in the divorce. I think she got far more than she deserved."

"She's claiming she's having a hard time, can't go back to work, and is on the brink of being evicted," Trevor said, his voice laced with mock fear.

"Don't let her fool you," Xavier growled, a girly laugh rumbling in his chest.

"Believe me, I won't," Trevor replied confidently.

"I have no sympathy for her or my father. Don't get me wrong, me and my father have pretty much made amends, but I will never completely forget the pain he brought to our family, especially to my mother. As for Rianna, that woman is just another power-hungry church lady. She's finally getting what she deserves." Xavier chuckled.

Trevor laughed too. "Well, look, I'm going to let you go. I have another meeting shortly, but I wanted to update you on the latest with Rianna."

"'Preciate it. But what about you? You good?" Xavier asked.

"Yeah, just trying to keep my head on straight. Niesha has all these wedding plans and I'm just trying to do what she says, man. But I tell you, it's a bit much. If it was left up to me, we would go to the courthouse and get married, but you already know she's not having that."

"I know. Y'all about to have the wedding of the year," Xavier teased. "But it's all good. I'm happy for you. Niesha seems cool. But I do wish she shared in your religious beliefs."

"Well, that's a hopeless cause. At least I think it is 'cause if you ask me, Niesha is an atheist. She doesn't call herself one, but she's definitely not into religion, and I'm cool with that. I'm not about trying to change another person. I love her regardless."

"As long as you're happy there's nothing more I can say," he said, his tone suddenly turning dry. "At least y'all aren't living a lie. You know who you are and what you want. I admire that."

15

"What about you? You still having problems at home?"

"Basically. I mean, it's the same ol' thing, bruh. It's not going to go away unless I do something to change it. You know, Pepper is a good mother. She tries to make me happy."

"But that's not enough, is it? Am I right?"

Xavier nodded. "Yeah, you are."

"Listen, I'm the last brotha that can tell you how to live your life, but what I can tell you is don't live your life regretting the decisions you've made. Especially decisions that are in your power to change. As for your marriage, all I can say is Pepper deserves to know the truth. If you're not feeling her, you're just not feeling her. It's not like she didn't know who she was getting married to. She knew your first choice when it came to relationships. But she didn't wanna hear that. So, if you realize it's not going to work, then you have to tell her, man. You at least owe her and yourself that truth. Don't carry this like a noose around your neck. It'll take you down unless you do something about it."

Xavier was silent but his facial expressions said a lot. "Thanks, man, but I don't know what I'm going to do just yet. I just know I have to do something. But I don't want to go down that road today. I have a lot on my mind as it is. I found what could be some major discrepancies in the church finances that I'm looking into. It's like trying to find a needle in a haystack. It's driving me up the wall. That, combined with the fact I need to make a decision about my life, is enough to make me want to get away from this place. Go someplace where nobody knows my name."

"Yeah, but you have your sons to think about. You can't just walk out on them."

"I know, right."

Xavier's administrative assistant appeared in his office doorway. "Mr. McCoy."

Xavier looked up from his phone.

"Oh, excuse me, I didn't know you were on a call," she said.

Xavier raised a hand. "No problem. I'm wrapping up," he said.

"Okay." The admin turned and walked away.

"Trevor, man, thanks for listening."

"You know I'm here for you. How can I not be? You're my friend...and one of my groomsmen."

They chuckled.

***

After the video chat, Trevor turned back to the files on his desk. He wondered what kind of discrepancies Xavier had found. Surely whatever it was had nothing to do with Hezekiah's finances. If that had been the case, wouldn't Xavier have said it?

Trevor dismissed thoughts of concern and instead mentally replayed Rianna's threat. For her sake, he hoped she wasn't foolish enough to delve into his personal affairs. That could lead to dangerous territory, for her, that is. As a precaution Trevor double-checked the hidden computer files, making sure everything remained secure.

Next, he reviewed the financial transactions he had carried out over the past few months. Since becoming Hezekiah McCoy's Power of Attorney, Trevor's personal wealth and bank account had significantly increased.

He had formed a partnership with his best friend, tax attorney M. J. Rease. Their partnership was swiftly turning out to be a match made in deceitful heaven.

Initially cautious, M.J. was won over by Trevor's cunning knowledge of the murky world of underhanded business dealings. Together, the best friends found a way to manipulate and siphon off Hezekiah's wealth with relative ease. Trevor only needed to keep Hezekiah in the dark about the gradual depletion of his substantial bank accounts until he and M.J. secured the properties and land they had set their sights on while also padding their bank accounts. After the wedding, he planned to get the heck out of dodge.

Trevor's fingers danced across the keyboard as he transferred more of Hezekiah's money into his accounts. He cackled with glee as the funds disappeared with a simple click of his mouse. It was like taking candy from a baby.

"Done," he exclaimed, spinning in his plush office chair. "Thank you, Hezekiah McCoy. Thank you very much." His maniacal laughter echoed throughout his home study like a cruel symphony of greed and treachery.

five

"When we are no longer able to change a situation, we are challenged to change ourselves." V. Frankl

Trevor was mid-bite, treasuring a juicy peach slice, when he abruptly stopped in his tracks. His eyes fixated on the television when he saw Pastor Stiles Graham standing on the steps of New Holy Rock Ministries talking to popular news reporter Jeremy Parker. At that moment, he was frozen, unable to swallow his mouthful of fruit, as he listened intently to Parker's live broadcast.

"We're in front of New Holy Rock Ministries where we are joined by interim senior pastor Stiles Graham. Pastor Graham, what can you tell us about the vandalism that occurred here last night?"

Stiles began, his voice thick with emotion. "We've been here almost four years with not one bit of trouble. Now, out of nowhere, we're faced with this devastating act."

"Do you know what happened?" Parker asked.

Stiles shook his head from side to side before answering. "Nah, but whoever did this came in through the windows on the back side of the church and once they were inside proceeded to wreak havoc."

Stiles' eyes welled up as he continued. "The equipment we use to broadcast our services was destroyed. Many of the pews and floors were drenched in bleach. Graffiti now covers the walls of our once-beautiful fellowship hall. It's an absolute disaster. It breaks my heart to see God's temple treated with such disrespect."

"You have no idea who could have done this?" the journalist pressed.

"No, I don't," replied Stiles, "but even amid this chaos, I'm reminded that nothing happens without God's permission. We will rise above this. We will overcome any obstacles the enemy throws our way."

The camera panned away from Stiles and zoomed back on the reporter.

"Thank you, Pastor Graham. Unfortunately, it appears New Holy Rock Ministries has experienced more than its share of tragedies. Not only is the church dealing with this recent act of vandalism, but this is the same church where founder and senior pastor, Reverend Hezekiah McCoy, was shot by the stepfather of his love child. In addition, McCoy is serving a 12-year prison sentence on child endangerment charges. At present, authorities are investigating the vandalism incident. Reporting live for News Channel 29 in Memphis, this is Jeremy Parker."

When the reporter ended his news segment, Trevor called Xavier. "Hey, did you hear what happened at New Holy Rock last night?"

"Hey, I was just reading about it on my timeline. I hate to be the one to say it, but looks like incarcerated or not, Pops still has enemies lurking. I just wonder who's responsible for doing the deed," said Xavier. "It's crazy, man."

"Yeah, it is. I could tell from his expression that your uncle is going through the roof about this. I can't begin to imagine what your father is going to say."

"I'll give Stiles a call and check on him. I guess I should be expecting a call from Pops any time now too. News travels fast in the joint, according to him. I wonder if Rianna could have something to do with it."

"I don't know. I hadn't thought about that. She *did* threaten to do something if she didn't get her way, but I don't think she would do something like this," Trevor added.

"I don't put anything past that woman."

"I hear you," Trevor remarked. "She is definitely a witch."

six

"Believe those who are seeking the truth. Doubt those who find it." Unknown

"Are you telling me they still don't have any leads?" Hezekiah demanded, leaning against the concrete wall with a sense of urgency. "It's been almost a month since it happened and they haven't caught anyone yet."

The beat-up wall phone he was talking on seemed to cling to life by a thin thread, as four other inmates impatiently waited their turn to use it.

"I can only tell you what they're telling me," replied Stiles. "I don't know if they're even making this a priority. I doubt it though. Black church, Black neighborhood. Nah, I don't think MPD is too bothered."

"Why does that not surprise me?" remarked Hezekiah, frowning and nervously rubbing his thinning head of hair.

"I've gone over the church security footage multiple times, but all we can see are two figures dressed head-to-toe in black. We can't make out anything other than that. They moved quickly."

"That's not good enough," Hezekiah pressed, his voice rising with frustration. "I want to know who did this. Don't let the police sweep this aside. We need answers. Did you call Xavier? He needs to contact our insurance adjusters."

"Don't worry, I've got it under control," Stiles assured him. "I left a message for Xavier."

"Call him again. Keep calling him. This needs to be taken care of now."

"I got it. Calm down," Stiles insisted. "Tell me, what's the latest on *your* situation? Any news?"

"No, not yet. Black is supposed to visit next week. I'm hoping he has some positive news because these hits I've been taking lately make it harder to keep standing," Hezekiah replied, desperation evident in his voice. "I'm sick of being stuck in this place. I need to get out of here. I'm not like Paul and Silas."

"Stay positive," Stiles encouraged. "Remember, God is always working. You know that. I understand that the encourager needs encouragement sometimes too. That's why I'm here—to do just that. As for Paul and Silas, God shook the foundations of the prison and immediately the doors were opened and everyone's bands were loosed. He did it for them and God can do the same for you. "

"Thanks, my brother," Hezekiah said, pausing for a moment. "Forgive me, Lord, for doubting your power."

It became increasingly evident that he carried deep emotional pain within him.

"Hey, you heard anything from that crazy ex of mine?" Hezekiah's voice abruptly shifted to a lighter tone. "Trevor told me she came to him demanding money. I told him he better not give her one red cent. I don't wish bad on anyone, but that's one chick if she was homeless, I'd pass her by."

"I heard that. Well, to answer your question, I haven't heard from her and I don't want to hear from her," Stiles replied adamantly, shaking his head. "There's enough going on already. I don't think I can deal with the likes of your ex-wife right now."

Hezekiah chuckled.

"Speaking of Trevor Price, you know he and Xavier have gotten close?"

"No, not really. I spoke to Xavier a couple of weeks ago. He sounded like he had a lot on his mind. I tried to get him to open up, but he wouldn't. H's always been like that. Closed off and hard to open up. What's up with him and Trevor? I hope none of that funny stuff," Hezekiah said.

"Nah, nothing funny is going on. I actually think Trevor could be good for him. He seems to accept Xavier for who he is. It's like Xavier has another brother," Stiles said, smiling. "I think Price is a good dude," Stiles noted. "He's got your back."

"Definitely," Hezekiah agreed. "And I'm glad he and Xavier get along. Trevor is a stand-up guy. I couldn't have made a better choice of a lawyer for my divorce, and he's been a godsend as my POA. He's even made me some money since he took over my finances. Besides you, he's the only other person I fully trust."

"Thanks, glad to hear that," Stiles replied. "I don't know if he told you but he joined New Holy Rock a few Sundays ago. You'll also be happy to know that Attorney Black and his wife said they're seriously thinking about becoming members too. I know Black is ready. He's just waiting on his wife to give him her approval. You know she has the final say." Stiles laughed.

A smile stretched across Hezekiah's face. "Thanks, man. I didn't know about Trevor, but yeah, Black told me he and his wife were going to join. I'm glad to know the church is thriving and reaching souls. I'm grateful, bruh. New Holy Rock would have gone under if it weren't for you. God knows what he's doing. I'll talk to you later. These guys behind me are getting anxious to use this phone."

"Okay, take it easy. I'll see you in a few weeks."

After the call ended, Stiles took a walk around New Holy Rock. His head lowered in disbelief and his heart grew heavy with hurt and disappointment as he eyed the disastrous mess and significant damage.

Two insurance adjusters arrived shortly after. They surveyed the damage and told

Stiles they would contact him in a few days with an estimate.

"Pastor...Pastor Stiles," the silver-haired woman said when Stiles walked outside to the back of the church.

Stiles was pleasantly surprised to see the woman he recognized as Mother Wilson, one of the members of New Holy Rock.

"Good morning, Mother Wilson. How are you?"

"Blessed and highly favored for an eighty-six-year-old."

Stiles chuckled. "You're getting younger and more beautiful every day."

Mother Wilson laughed.

"What can I do for you?"

"Pastor Stiles, I still can't believe someone would do something like this to the church," she said looking around at bits of remaining debris still scattered across the grounds. "I was out of town when it happened. I had to go to my baby brother's funeral."

"I was sorry to hear about your brother. The church has been praying for you and your family."

As if he hadn't said a word, Mother Wilson kept right on talking. "When I got back home, I saw something on my computer. I think you might want to see it. Come over to my house if you have time. I'll show it to you."

"I have some time now."

Stiles accompanied the woman to her bungalow-styled home, unsure of just what it was she was determined to show him. He didn't put up a fuss. He loved his members

26

and there was nothing he wouldn't do for them, especially his older members like Mother Wilson.

"Come in the den," she ordered. "It's on my computer. You young folk know how to show this stuff on your phones, but it's easier for me to see it on my computer. My eyes aren't what they used to be, especially when I'm trying to pull up stuff on that cell phone."

"I understand," he replied, trailing Mother Wilson through her immaculate home and into the den.

She turned on the computer and went to the security camera app.

"I didn't think much about it at first, but then I remembered somebody broke into the church. I looked at it again and that's when I knew I had to tell you. I'm so glad I wasn't home when it happened. I live alone, and whoever did it could have done something to me or any of the other seniors in this neighborhood."

Stiles watched the video several times. The short clip was too grainy to see much of anything clearly, but he could make out two people, possibly women, standing next to a car a couple of houses from Mother Wilson's house. He had a feeling it was Rianna and her friend. He couldn't be a hundred percent certain, but then again who else would want to destroy New Holy Rock besides Rianna McCoy?

The church camera only captured the surrounding exterior of the building.

"Thank you for showing me this, Mother Wilson. If it's okay with you, I'd like to make a copy. I think we need to show it to the police."

"You go right ahead. Make as many copies as you need to. I just appreciate you, and the church too. It was a blessing when y'all moved into this neighborhood. God bless you, baby. Y'all have helped me so much. The Landscape Ministry keeps my yard cut. The Kitchen Ministry delivers a hot meal twice a week. Yes, it's been a blessing. That's why I just don't understand folks these days. Tearing up the church? Lord, have mercy on whoever did such a thing."

Stiles gave Mother Wilson a tight embrace and a light peck on her wrinkled cheek. "I need to get going. And don't you worry, Mother Wilson, the church is going to keep looking out for you and the other seniors in this neighborhood. Take care."

seven

"I have learned how to hold my temper for a long while. I just haven't mastered controlling it once it blows." J. Weatherhead

The atmosphere in the room was tense as Stiles delivered a fiery outburst directed at Rianna.

"Do you know how long it's going to take to rebuild what you and those thugs destroyed in a matter of minutes? What is wrong with you? How could you do something like this? Whoever you convinced to go along with your madness is going to pay, but even if I never find out who they are, you can be sure of this one thing—you, Rianna Jamison, are going to pay for your evil deeds," he yelled, his tone full of rage. "Believe me, if I have anything to do with it, you're going away for a long time. You are a wolf all dolled up in sheep's clothing. You never meant Hezekiah any good. And now you

do something like this? What is wrong with
you?"

Stiles slammed his fist on the wooden
corner table, his eyes ablaze with anger as he
confronted Rianna inside Apartment 3D.

Rianna's face twisted in fear as she
protested her innocence. "I'm telling you, I
didn't do it!" she cried, her voice shaking with
emotion. "That is not me, or Tiny, or her car, in
that video. Did that punk attorney Trevor Price
tell you I did it? If he did, he's a liar. That man
is evil. He's out to get me. I think Hezekiah is
paying him to make my life miserable."

Stiles was not swayed. "This has nothing to
do with Trevor Price. I know what I saw." Stiles
chuckled, almost shoving his phone in her
face. "You see here. You were almost out of
view, but that's you," he pointed to the video.
"And I bet on my life this is your friend
standing on the side of that car. Look."

"That is not me! I don't care what you say."
Rianna folded her arms and leaned slightly
against the sofa.

"I don't know who those thugs were who
vandalized the church, but this is you. I know
it is."

"Think what you want to think," Rianna
said smugly.

"Will you take a lie detector test?"

Rianna was stunned. Her eyes bulged in her
head. "A lie detector test? Are you kidding me?"
she huffed, her jaws suddenly tight.

"I thought so," Stiles said, nodding.

Tears suddenly streamed down her face. Rianna cried, "I didn't do it. That is not me in that video and it ain't Tiny either!"

Stiles remained unfazed. "You're lying," he spat, storming towards the door of Apartment 3D. "But we'll let the law decide if it's you or not," he fumed.

Rianna's hands flew to her mouth in shock when Stiles yanked the door open and bolted out. She closed and locked the door before rushing to where her cell phone lay on the table next to the sofa.

Pushing buttons with trembling fingers, she called Tiny.

Tiny answered, sounding like she'd been awakened from sleep.

"Tiny, oh Tiny. I'm sorry," she cried.

"Sorry? Whatchu talkin' 'bout?" Tiny asked, suddenly sounding awake and alert.

"Stiles," Rianna cried.

"Stiles? You talkin' about Pastor Graham?"

"Yes, who else would I be talkin' about?"

"What about him? Spit it out. What are you talkin' about?"

"He knows. He knows it was us outside the church. He has us on a video. It's not clear, but I'm still scared. They can do all sorts of things to make those images clearer, you know. Oh, Tiny, I'm scared," she repeated. "He said he's going to the police."

On the other end of the phone, Tiny's voice quivered as the weight of her involvement in Rianna's latest mess seemed to suddenly dawn on her. Overwhelmed by the realization of what

31

she had allowed herself to become mixed up in, she lashed out at her best friend.

"What have you done now? Oh, God, I can't go to jail. Not again, 'specially not because of something that wasn't even my fault. I can't. I could lose my son. I could lose everything. I shoulda known betta. I shoulda stayed my behind at home that night!"

"I'm sorry, Tiny," Rianna cried. "Please forgive me. I didn't mean for any of this to happen. I swear I didn't."

"I don't believe you and I sure don't trust you. Not anymore. Oh, God, please don't let me lose my son. I can't....I hate you for this, Rianna. I hate you for making me a part of your messed up life. Leave me alone. Just freaking leave me alone!"

The phone went silent.

Rianna's sobs filled the room as she cried into her hands. With the clock ticking, she was left to face the consequences of her actions. The fate of her future hung in the balance, and she had no idea what the outcome would be.

eight

"I have things in my head that would scare you off in a heartbeat; and things that would addict you to me for eternity." J. Weatherhead

The cozy lanai was awash with a warm glow, thanks to the flickering candlelight and the rich orange and brown tones of the teakwood loveseat they were snuggled on. The Memphis night air was unseasonably mild to be the end of winter, but Trevor and Niesha were too lost in each other to notice.

"Heads up, sweetheart, I have to make the long drive to Bledsoe tomorrow morning. I need to see my client before I go off the radar these next three weeks. I can't let anything mess up our wedding and honeymoon." Trevor moaned and Niesha gasped as he pulled her close, crashing his lips into hers.

Niesha purred when their lips parted, looping her smooth legs around Trevor's jean-clad thighs. "You want me to go with you? I know that drive can be a drag."

"Of course I want you to go, but I thought you had a mountain of pre-wedding tasks you wanted to tackle," Trevor replied.

"True, but what's a maid of honor for if not to lend a hand to the bride?" Niesha said with a cheeky grin.

Trevor planted another soft kiss on her black bobbed hair and chuckled. "No way, sweetheart. You stay here and take care of business. I won't be the one responsible for you sulking down the aisle because we missed a deadline."

With that, he tightened his arm around her, pulling her even closer as she melted against him.

†

The following morning, as Trevor embarked on the journey to Bledsoe Correctional Facility, the monotony of the road ahead loomed. An hour into the drive, he felt a pang of regret that Niesha hadn't joined him. Her infectious laughter and whimsical Tik-Tok reenactments would have made this long, lonely stretch of road bearable. However, she had important wedding preparations to attend to, as their nuptials was just days away.

Today's visit was not going to be just another ordinary visitation. Armed with fake bank statements and transactions, Trevor was determined to convince Hezekiah that all was going well and that he would see him after he returned from his honeymoon.

Trevor's pulse quickened and he exhaled as the towering walls of Bledsoe came into view. He was ready to push his cunning plan further into motion and leave no stone unturned.

With a sly grin, he turned into the prison, his mind filled with memories of his shrewd deal with M. J., a decision that had launched the friends on a path toward wealth and success. Their new business acquiring residential and commercial property and land was flourishing at an astonishing rate. It was easy to cover up and the perfect way to cipher funds from Hezekiah's assets.

Trevor was determined to seize every opportunity and make the most of his future. His thirst for the good life was unquenchable, and he couldn't wait to see what more good fortune lay ahead.

†

"How's your appeal coming along? Have you heard from your attorney?" Trevor asked during his visit.

"According to him, it's looking favorable. I hope so, I can't stay in here much longer," Hezekiah replied, sighing. "Things are getting wilder every day. These young bucks don't have regard for anything or nobody. They'll make a man like me lose it. I'm telling you, I have to get out of here!"

"Just hold on. Christian Black is supposed to be one of the best. If anyone can get you out of here, I heard he can," Trevor said, trying to reassure him.

"Yeah, I keep telling myself that, but we'll see."

"Here are your latest bank statements. I put more money on your books, too," Trevor said as he handed over the envelope full of documents.

"Thanks." Hezekiah briefly peeped inside and scanned the statements. "I'll go over them when I get back to my cell. I appreciate you, man," Hezekiah said.

"Hey, that's what you pay me for," Trevor replied with a grin.

"So, you're about to put on the old ball and chain, huh?" Hezekiah chuckled, raising an eyebrow.

"Yep, tying that knot."

"Just don't make the same mistake I did. I've said 'I do' twice and look where it got me. Divorced and locked up," Hezekiah chuckled as he leaned back in his chair.

"I think I have a winner. She has my back, or so it seems," Trevor said, shrugging.

"You're going out of the country for your honeymoon?" Hezekiah asked.

"Yeah, that's why I made sure you have plenty of funds for your commissary," Trevor replied.

"Thanks, I appreciate it."

"Oh, yeah, and happy belated birthday. I know you didn't plan on spending another birthday in here, but things could be worse," Trevor said, reaching across the table and patting Hezekiah's shoulder.

"Yeah, guess I could be six feet under, although I do feel like a dead man walking in this place." Hezekiah started rubbing his head back and forth.

"Hang in there. Things are going to get easier."

"I keep telling myself that."

"Guess I better go. I have to make that drive. Is there anything you need me to do?" Trevor asked as he rose from his seat.

"Nah, I'm good. I wish you the best," Hezekiah said as he stood up too and shook Trevor's hand.

"Oh, yeah, before I go, did you hear?" Trevor asked, pausing at the door.

"Hear what?" Hezekiah scowled.

"I think there might be trouble brewing on the homefront. He called the other day. He's thinking about getting out of the marriage. Said he doesn't know how much more he can take," Trevor said, lowering his voice.

"Xavier?"

"Yes."

"Dang, I hate to hear that. We talked a few days ago. He didn't mention anything about having problems. Then again, we were caught up talking about discrepancies he found with the church finances," Hezekiah said, looking concerned. "I hope he and his wife can work it out. He has a family now. He doesn't need to go and do anything rash."

"I told him we'd talk some more when I get back from my honeymoon. It's a tough predicament for him, especially when kids are involved," Trevor said, sympathetically.

"Thanks for letting me know."

"No problem. Look, you take it easy. I'll see you when I get back to the States."

"Wait, I was meaning to ask if you've heard anything else from Rianna."

"No, not since I told her she wasn't getting any more money from you," Trevor replied.

"Good. I wish she'd go somewhere and disappear."

Walking from around the table, the men gave each other a quick hug and pat on the back.

"Congrats again, Trevor." Hezekiah turned and looked at the guard. "You can take me back to my cell," he barked.

nine

"Our love is like a song that only we can hear."
Unknown

Trevor's text notifier chimed and interrupted his thoughts.

"U almost home?"

He smiled and slightly shook his head before quickly texting, "About 35 min away, can't talk. I'm driving"

He ignored the next text chime and continued driving. He couldn't wait to get home and chill. The next few days would be busy with his approaching wedding. He thought about some of the things he and Hezekiah talked about, particularly about relationships. One thing he had learned about Hezekiah, he was always eager to dispense advice. Most of the time it was considered good advice even though he was known to do some ungodly things.

A whirlwind of thoughts invaded Trevor's headspace as he pondered his life. He was days from getting married, but he couldn't shake the feeling of uncertainty. Had they known each other long enough for him to make a lifetime commitment? As if that wasn't enough to cause him to worry, Trevor grappled with the guilt of his actions as Hezekiah's POA. Nonetheless, he was never a stranger to breaking rules.

When he was a kid, and before his mother walked out of his life, he liked playing *pranks* on his parents. As an only child, he was always finding ways to push their buttons. If they said go left, he went right.

Sometimes Trevor blamed himself and those awful pranks for his mother leaving, but it didn't stop him. Instead, his pranks escalated into him doing more sinister things.

When he became a teenager, he dabbled in petty thievery like shoplifting and stealing from school lockers and backpacks. He had an insatiable desire for taking risks, good or bad. Somehow, he always managed to evade being caught.

As an adult and successful practicing attorney, his penchant for risky activities had only intensified.

He still managed to avoid getting caught doing anything illegal, but some of his decisions were starting to weigh on him.

Despite his moral shortcomings, Trevor had true admiration for his father, who had been a respected attorney with a strong sense of integrity and character up until he died.

Trevor, on the other hand, was driven by his desire to have lots of money and plenty of power. He was well on his way. He told himself he was cut from a different cloth than his father. He was nobody's pushover. His father would give people the benefit of the doubt, the shirt off his back.

Trevor witnessed more than once how his father's kindness backfired. There were occasions when clients and friends took advantage of his father's generosity, meaning more often, his bank account. He was not going to be like his father in that instance.

With this new opportunity and partnership with M. J., Trevor saw his chance and he took it. Doors that would have taken years to open, were opening faster than he could turn the key. He wasn't going to let it slip away.

He used Hezekiah's money to buy land and property in the U.S. and overseas. On his honeymoon to Morocco, he was going to check out several small shops and businesses that he'd reviewed online. He planned to open a trendy shop, or shops, on the beach in Morocco with Niesha by his side.

Though he knew he was treading on dangerous ground, Trevor still felt an adrenaline rush of excitement at the possibilities that lay ahead. All he had to do was make sure to keep Niesha from finding out about his dark side.

He finally pulled into his driveway. When he saw Niesha's car parked on the street, he smiled. His smile was replaced with a wide yawn. He got out of his car and trudged to the door.

Opening the front door, he dragged himself inside, releasing yet another yawn.

"Come here and let me make it all better," Niesha said, appearing from around the corner dressed in one of his oversized tees. Sliding up next to him, she wrapped her arms around his neck and pulled him in for a deep, wet kiss.

"Hey there," he said, his voice strained, inhaling the sweet smell of her skin. He wanted to go fall across his bed but he couldn't turn her down. He never could. She was like a drug he couldn't get enough of. He devoured her lips while raking his hands feverishly up and down her skimpily clad body.

"Come on," she whispered, pulling away from him and grabbing hold of his hand. "I know you want to take a hot shower. I'll help you," she cooed, leading him around the corner to his bathroom. "Don't worry about a thing. Niesha poo is going to take real good care of you."

ten

*"Fall in love with someone who doesn't make
you think love is hard." Unknown*

Trevor's wedding day had arrived. The
bright, airy wedding venue was known for
hosting some of the Mid-south's most elegant
and prestigious events. The ballroom exuded
an air of elegance and sophistication. An
abundance of natural light streamed through
large windows. Sparkling crystal chandeliers,
suspended from the ceiling, cast a shimmering
glow, kissing every corner. Every detail,
including the meticulously crafted floral
arrangements, was tailored to create memories
the couple, and their guests, could cherish for
a lifetime.

Trevor stood outside the atrium along with
five, gray tuxedo-wearing groomsmen by his
side. His nervousness showed to the point a
couple of the groomsmen poked fun at him.

"Man, you look like one of those fellows posted outside Buckingham Palace," one of them said, laughing. "Look at dude!"

M. J., his best man, added to the teasing. "You look like you just saw a ghost. Your face is red as a beet. You all right, my brother?"

"Yeah, I'm just wondering where ol' boy is. If he doesn't show up, one of the bridesmaids won't have an escort. Niesha is going to be pissed," Trevor said.

"I'm sure he'll turn up. He probably got caught in traffic or something. Anyway, the wedding planner will figure it out. That's not for you to worry about," M.J. said.

"Yeah, listen to your best man. Just concentrate on getting married," said another groomsman.

Trevor nodded. His groomsmen were right. He couldn't be concerned about why Xavier hadn't shown up. He had tried calling him several times and each call went to voicemail. The string of text messages went unanswered as well. When Xavier attended the rehearsal dinner, he didn't say he had a problem or that he wasn't going to be a groomsman. Something was off. Trevor didn't know what it was. But as his friends said, today was his wedding day. Anything other than making it down that aisle and saying I do to Niesha was irrelevant.

"Y'all are right. And I'm good. I'm ready to do this," he said, taking one last look in the massive atrium mirror to check his attire.

The uncertainty plastered on Trevor's face when the doors to the ballroom opened quickly disappeared and overwhelming love and gratitude filled his heart, almost making him tearful. On this day he was not only marrying the love of his life but also making a statement of his devotion and commitment to her. Thanks to the extra money he was raking in, he had chosen to personally foot the bill for the extravagant wedding, instead of following tradition and having the bride's parents pay. This was another way of showing his unwavering love and dedication to Niesha.

"Trevor, do you take this woman to be your wedded wife?" the officiator said.

"I do."

As they exchanged their vows in front of 150 guests, sitting among a stunning formal setting of crisp white pews and polished tiled floors, Trevor felt like the luckiest man in the world. He hoped this was the beginning of a lifetime of love and happiness.

✝

Sharing their first dance as husband and wife, the thought of starting a new life across the ocean filled Trevor with a sense of excitement mixed with apprehension. Could he live happily ever after with Niesha? Would marriage work for him? Would he be able to get away with what he was doing or would justice catch up to him?

The unknown added an air of mystery and intrigue to Trevor's future. Leaving behind his practice, his friends, and his family would be the biggest risk he'd taken in his life. His emotions were all over the place.

On the one hand, he felt like he had won the lottery, despite the fact he was lining his pockets with his client's money. On another hand, he was definitely feeling invincible and on top of the world. However, he couldn't seem to shake the nagging feeling that there had to be consequences for his actions. Yet, who would ultimately pay the price? Certainly, it wouldn't be him and shouldn't be him. After all, he could always argue that he was making the decisions he made for the benefit and at the request of his client. It is no secret, he would argue, that Hezekiah McCoy wanted a POA who would invest and take the risks he would take if he was a free man. When he thought of it in that way, Trevor pushed aside the tidbits of guilt that tried to nibble away at his mind. He convinced himself that if anyone deserved payback it was Hezekiah McCoy and not him.

Hezekiah had mistreated and made a fool of a lot of people, especially his first wife, Fancy. Yep, if anybody deserved to be on the chopping block, it was Hezekiah McCoy. So, in that case, if anything *did* go down, Trevor was going to do everything in his power to make sure it was Hezekiah, and not him, who took the fall.

eleven

"We all have stories that we will not tell."
HeretoInspire

The two weeks spent in Morocco proved to be the adventure of a lifetime. From indulging in their luxurious honeymoon suite to exploring the ornate mosques and structures, Trevor and Niesha's days were filled with romantic bliss and new discoveries.

Trevor was in awe of seeing the bustling streets of Morocco come alive with a symphony of sights, sounds, and scents. The irresistible allure of Morocco's charm enticed him to relocate there with even greater force.

Outdoor markets pulsed with energy, from grand bazaars like Rue des Consuls in the capital city of Rabat to the electrifying Jamaa el Fna in Marrakech, where the city transformed into a nighttime extravaganza filled with snake charmers, acrobats, and other captivating performers.

In Casablanca, fine dining and lively entertainment made for an unforgettable experience, leaving an indelible mark on Trevor's heart.

The immensely rewarding journey he encountered during his stay surpassed his wildest imagination. No longer were his dreams limited to the distant images he'd seen only through YouTube videos, photos, and stories. With newfound appreciation, he saw himself and Niesha building a life and starting a family in this African oasis, free from the fear of extradition, making it that much more enticing.

Niesha, being the seasoned traveler, was more than willing to experience the country and show him the way. It would be easy for her to live here. She'd done it before, for a short period, and she was ready and willing to do it again if it would make Trevor happy.

†

Trevor returned to the office slightly tanned and with a skip in his step, fresh from the honeymoon of a lifetime. Little did his law associates know, Trevor had a grand plan up his sleeve. All he needed to do was settle the divorce cases he had coming up and transfer more money from Hezekiah's accounts to an overseas account.

As he settled back into his office, his phone dinged with a warm welcome from M. J. They made plans to have lunch at Eve's Diner, where juicy gossip was served alongside Eve's famous cheesesteak hoagies.

Over lunch, M. J. dropped a bombshell. "Rianna McCoy was allegedly caught on camera along with some goons vandalizing New Holy Rock."

Trevor nearly choked on his food with laughter at the sheer idiocy of the situation. "Are you serious?" he responded, still trying to catch his breath.

"Yep, as serious as a heart attack." M. J. chuckled. "If you're talking about leaving a trail of breadcrumbs for the cops to follow, that video did it!"

"Well, well, well. Bless her little sneaky, conniving heart." Trevor laughed harder. "Is she locked up?"

"I don't know. I didn't bother to look into that."

"I'll have to check it out," Trevor said, still laughing at the absurdity of it all. "Have you heard anything from Xavier? I still can't reach him. But I only tried once while I was in Morocco," he confessed. "There was too much fun being had while I was over there. I didn't have time to think about Xavier and his problems."

"I haven't heard from him either, but then again, he's your friend, not mine. Plus, you know what the old folks say. No news is good news."

"Still, it's not like him. I called his phone a few times since I've been back, but it's not in service. His text messages go unanswered too."

"Have you called his wife?" asked M.J.

"Nah, I thought about calling her but decided I'd better not. With me knowing he's having some marital discord, I didn't think it would be a good idea. I don't want to stir up trouble. Know what I mean?"

"Yeah, I understand. Hey, what about church? Don't y'all go to the same church?"

"Yeah, we do, but I can't say whether he's been to church or not. I'm just getting back to the States. But either way, you know I'm not one of those people that's at the church every time the door opens. Going every once in a while is enough for me."

"Maybe he had to get away for a minute or something," said M. J.

"Maybe, but to miss my wedding. Without a word?"

"I thought you said you got a text from him."

"My bad, you're right, I did. He texted a few minutes before me and Niesha boarded our plane for Morrocco. But the wedding was over. That was weird too because he texted from an unknown phone number. He had to let me know it was him. That only left me with more questions 'cause all he said was he was sorry he couldn't make it, congratulations, and he would get with me later and explain. Haven't heard a word since."

"You think he's on to what we got going on? You said he's a financial genius."

"Nah. He may be a genius when it comes to numbers and such, but he still hates what he's doing. Or that's what he tells me. He's only working at New Holy Rock because it's what's expected of him. It was either stay at Holy Rock or join *New* Holy Rock. Either way, he's not pleased with what you might call his lot in life," Trevor said, displaying air quotes. "Dude is definitely unhappy."

"I hate it for him. As for him knowing our business, I hope you're right about that. We're stacking this paper, man. We don't need him to come across anything we're doing. Our paper trail has to remain flawless. Keep in mind, at the end of the day, this is his daddy we're scheming. You say he's already loyal to his family, so I don't want any slip-ups. That's all," said M. J.

"He hasn't had access to his daddy's financial accounts since I became POA. If that *was* the case, I think he would have said something. I'm confident, we got all our bases covered."

"Okay, then I'm telling you, it sounds like dude went ghost. The ol' girl was probably nagging him 'til he couldn't take any more. He needed a break. Man, that's why I'm single— I'ma stay that way too." M. J. laughed.

After chatting about Rianna and Xavier for a few more minutes, Trevor switched to more personal matters.

"You know, M.J., man, I want to let you know that you're more than a business partner, more than my best friend, you're like a brother to me."

"Same here, but what's up? Why are you getting all sentimental on me?"

"I'm just stating facts. Speaking of business partners, are you sure you'll be able to keep things in check? I'll be overseas, out of physical reach, living in a foreign land. How are we going to handle situations that may come up?"

"Have no fear," M. J. assured him. "With modern technology, we'll be able to stay in touch. But regardless of whether near or far, we always need to be careful in our communication when it comes to discussing and transacting business."

"Indeed," Trevor agreed. "As long as we keep our dealings under wraps, there's nothing to worry about."

M. J. nodded in agreement.

M. J. was the only person Trevor trusted to take care of their affairs while he embarked on his journey to Morocco. With M. J.'s reliable hand guiding their business in the states, Trevor was confident life was about to take a huge turn, all in his favor and all thanks to Hezekiah McCoy's funding.

twelve

"A pretty face is nothing if you have an ugly heart."
Unknown

The ominous knock echoed through the stillness of Rianna's apartment. She cautiously approached the peephole and peered through to find two stern-faced officers from the Memphis Police Department on the other side, striking fear into her heart. With a lump in her throat and shivers running up and down her spine, she slowly opened the door, greeting the officers with a trembling voice.

"Rianna McCoy?" one of the officers asked, his unwavering tone leaving no room for doubt of who she was.

"Yes?" she stammered, her voice barely audible.

"We need you to come with us to the police station to answer some questions regarding an act of vandalism that took place at New Holy Rock Ministries last month," the second officer stated, his eyes cold and unyielding.

"I don't understand. What does that have to do with me?" Rianna asked, her fear mounting with each passing moment. "I don't know anything about that."

She moved back a step and almost tumbled over the ocean blue chair she had bought Hezekiah as a birthday gift shortly after they first started their relationship.

"I, I don't know what I can tell you."

Despite her weak protests of innocence, the officers were relentless.

"Just come with us," the shorter officer insisted.

†

After hours of intense police interrogation, Rianna was left reeling from the traumatic experience.

"Have a good night, ma'am," one of the officers said as they drove her back to her apartment. "It's still a possibility that you'll be picked up again for questioning, so don't make plans to leave town anytime soon."

Back inside the sanctity of Apartment 3D, Rianna lay immobilized on her rumpled bed, surrounded by the cluttered and disheveled state of her once tidy space. The weight of potential prison time hung over her head as she faced the daunting realities of her uncertain future.

The mere thought of tending to basic household chores seemed impossible, especially in the face of the emotional turmoil she was grappling with. This intensified her overwhelming feelings of fear, depression, and anxiety. Her living space was now a reflection of the inner turmoil she was struggling to overcome.

Days later, desperate for help, Rianna turned to a public defender, who offered her a glimmer of hope.

"Mrs. McCoy, I believe I can confidently say it's literally impossible to tell who this is," carefully studying the video. "It's too hard to say this is you and your uh, your friend."

"That's what I tried to tell the police and that's what I'm telling you. It's not us," she insisted.

The public defender eyed her curiously. He had seen his share of innocent and guilty people to the point he could tell when someone was lying or when they were telling the truth. The woman sitting across from him, looking like she had lost her life's savings, was definitely lying.

"Mrs. McCoy, let me be clear. Being honest is key to any partnership we may have. If you want me to even consider taking your case, that is, if you are even charged with a crime, I expect you to tell me the truth at all times. I cannot fairly represent you if you lie to me. Do you understand?"

Rianna nodded, staring blankly ahead. The weight of the consequences of her reckless choices was becoming all too real.

"I understand, and I swear I'll tell you the truth. Just keep me from going to jail."

"I'll do my best if it comes to that. Do you know if they have apprehended the suspects that allegedly carried out the actual vandalism?"

"No, not that I know of," she whispered.

She would never say, but she knew the men she had paid to carry out the crime had not been apprehended, and from what she heard there were no leads. She hoped they would *never* be found. Just like the homeless guy she had paid to set fire to Fancy's house, these were just two more homeless men she had lured with the promise of a hearty meal and a few dollars. They had probably long left the area, possibly the city.

The gravity of the situation was not lost on Rianna, and she was now forced to accept her fate, starting with the shattered friendship between her and Tiny.

Tiny had made it clear that she wanted nothing else to do with her. Rianna couldn't blame her. What kind of friend would do her the way Rianna had done Tiny? There was no one else she could call on. Even Big Daddy wouldn't respond to her calls or texts. Then again, why would he? He had cut off all communication with her well over a year ago.

Her thoughtless actions, fueled by a desire for revenge, had led her down a path of self-destruction. As she reflected on her choices, the full extent of the damage she had caused became all too clear. Rianna was alone, with no one to turn to, and the haunting reality of her fate was rapidly closing in.

thirteen

"In order to form an immaculate member of a flock of sheep one must, above all, be a sheep." Einstein

The call from an MPD officer that evening offered Rianna the news she had been longing to hear. The emotional turmoil she had faced over the past eight weeks, compounded by her financial struggles had reached its climax.

"Ms. McCoy," the female officer spoke sternly, "I want to inform you that you have been cleared as a suspect in the vandalism of New Holy Rock. If you have any new information that could aid in our investigation, please contact us."

Rianna's face lit up with a smile, her still slightly scarred skin glowing with relief.

"Thank you, God. I've been telling y'all along that I had nothing to do with the vandalism of that church. Neither did my friend. You cleared her too, right?" Rianna asked eagerly.

"Yes, someone has already spoken to your friend. Have a good evening." The officer ended the call abruptly, leaving Rianna elated.

Next, Rianna attempted to call Tiny, only to be met with a message that the number was no longer in service. Had Tiny changed her number?

As she ended the call, her phone rang. It was Stiles.

"I don't know how you did it, but you're not getting away with it," he screamed with such force that Rianna could imagine saliva flying from his mouth.

Rianna laughed. "Come on, it's not that serious, brotha-n-law."

"Oh, so you think this is funny?"

"What's funny is you calling me shouting and screaming like somebody crazy."

"I'll show you crazy. That video may not have been enough to lock you up, but I know you did it, and I won't give up until I can prove it."

"Stiles, please. I told you from the jump it wasn't me, or Tiny, or her car, in that video. But *nooo*, you wouldn't listen. Hah, who looks like boo-boo the fool now?" She continued laughing.

"This isn't over. Remember, Rianna, vengeance is mine says the Lord.

"Boy, please. You don't scare me. You talk about God's vengeance, but clearly, God knows something you don't because I'm in the clear, baby!" Rianna hung up the phone and erupted into a fit of laughter.

Placing the phone on the end table, she headed to the kitchen and got a bottle of soda. She ambled over to the living room chair, sat down, and placed the soda on the table next to her.

The loss of Tiny's friendship weighed on Rianna. Tiny hadn't responded to any of her texts or calls and Rianna had given up trying to make amends with her best friend, until tonight when Rianna got the phone call from MPD.

Rianna had a history of damaging the relationships that mattered most to her. She had now done the same to her friendship with Tiny.

Growing up in a dysfunctional home plus in and out of the foster care system had taken its toll, leaving her with some serious and emotional trauma.

"If that's how you want to do it, then go right ahead. Do you, Tiny." She shrugged. "There're plenty of *Tinys* in this world, sweetie pie. You aren't the first and you certainly won't be the last."

Rianna swallowed another mouthful of soda, while she basked in the freedom that had eluded her the past eight weeks.

fourteen

"The heart is deceitful above all and beyond cure. Who can understand it." Jeremiah 17:9 The Bible

Trevor always had a plan B in place in case things took an unlikely turn. He had dropped a bombshell on his colleagues by announcing his plans to take an indefinite sabbatical from work.

Fast forward eight weeks, he was now a newlywed, armed with a hefty amount of money and a burning desire for adventure. Together with his bride, Trevor was eager to break free from the monotony of everyday life and embark on a journey of self-discovery. His heart yearned for the vibrant and exotic land of Morocco, where he saw endless possibilities to start a new chapter in his life and explore the world with unbridled curiosity and zeal.

He gave his office one last sweep to make sure he wasn't leaving anything important behind. He had no idea when or if he would ever return to this practice, or even to Tennessee. A rush of excitement came over him when he thought about the unknown future that lay ahead.

Saying a final farewell to his colleagues, he left and headed to M. J.'s office. M. J. was going to keep Trevor's Range Rover and he was going to drive Trevor and Niesha to the airport.

Cruising up the street through the rows of breathtaking maple trees lining each side of the road, Trevor exhaled as he thought about the big move he was about to make.

Once inside M. J.'s office, the two discussed the logistics of how their business would operate while Trevor was overseas.

"I don't foresee any problems out of the ordinary, at least nothing we shouldn't be able to handle with a phone call or text," M. J. reassured Trevor. "So far everything is running smoothly. You *are* still going to revoke the POA, right?"

"Yes, probably in the next six months or so. I want me and Niesha to be settled in Morocco and I want to have the first beach hut in full operation. Once that's done, I'll request to be removed as his POA."

"See, sounds like you have everything in place. All you need to do is enjoy your new life. Experience everything living in a new country has to offer. I mean, think about it. It's not like we're doing something bad, not really. We're doing like a lot of guys do these days."

"Yep, buying real estate, fixing it up, and flipping it."

"On part of the acreage we bought, we're building the nonprofit space and the rest of it we have plans to lease. Construction should start on that project in a couple of weeks. I say everything looks as it should."

"So, hey, we're legit, at least ninety-nine and a half percent," Trevor pointed out.

The guys laughed.

"Yep, definitely," M. J. added, chuckling.

"You know what?" said Trevor.

"What's up?" remarked M. J.

"I'm going to do as you suggested. I'm going to enjoy life, open those beach huts, and be happy with my gorgeous bride, in a beautiful country."

"Good for you, but I have to admit, I *am* a little jealous."

"No need. You're welcome to visit any time. You might get over there and meet you a little Moroccan hottie," Trevor teased.

"I'm all for that," M. J. shot back.

They left M. J.'s office and scooped up Niesha from her parents' home.

Arriving at the airport, Trevor said his goodbyes to M. J. before he and Niesha went inside.

M. J. watched as his friend and colleague disappeared through the airport doors before he got into his vehicle and headed back to the office. As he drove, he felt a pang of jealousy. Trevor was about to embark on a life that many people could only dream of. The thought of leaving the daily grind behind, traveling the world, and starting a new adventure was appealing to M. J. He admired Trevor's courage and determination to follow his dreams and make a fresh start, even if it was made possible with Hezekiah's money.

Nonetheless, despite the wrong they were doing, M. J. was happy for his friend, yet at the same time, M. J. was content with the life he had built for himself. He had a great career, a supportive circle of friends, and thanks to Trevor including him in his little venture, a fast-growing bank account.

Pulling into the office parking lot, he smiled at the thought of Trevor and Niesha's new life. He couldn't wait to hear all about their adventures and see pictures of the beautiful beach huts Trevor planned to build. M. J. believed that their friendship would continue, no matter where their lives took them.

†

Settling into his business-class seat, Trevor braced himself for the 18-hour flight. After sharing a tender kiss with Niesha, he leaned back into the soft, inviting cloth seats and closed his eyes followed by a sigh.

With a cunning plan in place, he was sure that everything would go according to his and M. J.'s masterful scheme. His mission, for now, was to keep an unsuspecting Hezekiah in the dark while they made the final, shadowy moves necessary to secure the rest of the money they would need to fully finance their business ventures and amass a small fortune. Then, with the flick of a pen, Trevor would revoke the power of attorney and live happily in Morocco.

If Your Price Is Right

Life was a thrilling game with endless, lucrative possibilities. Or was it?

Continue with the next short story, "Love Shoulda Brought You Home"

Words from the Author

~Holy Rock Chronicles Shorts~

This captivating behind-the-scenes collection of short stories continues to reveal new insights to me with each installment.

Although these are fictional characters, they are not so different from us. We all have our imperfections and flaws, and we all experience the ups and downs of life. But it's not about falling, it's about picking ourselves up and striving for redemption. Even when life doesn't go as planned, we can always find a way to make things right again.

So, take heart and travel this literary journey with me. Together, we'll explore the imperfect but relatable lives of the McCoys and the Grahams, and perhaps discover something new about ourselves along the way.

And always remember, these are "Perfect Stories About Imperfect People Like You....and Me!"

Shelia E. Bell
God's Amazing Girl!

More Perfect Stories About Imperfect People Like You...and Me

<u>*My Son's Wife Series*</u>
My Son's Wife: The Beginning (Book 1)
My Son's Ex-Wife: Aftershock (Book 2)
My Son's Next Wife (Book 3)
My Sister My Momma My Wife (Book 4)
My Wife My Baby...And Him (Book 5)
The McCoys of Holy Rock (Book 6)
Dem McCoy Boys (Book 7)
My Brother, Father...And Me (Book 8)
My Truth, My Time, My Turn (Book 9)
Dem Folk at Holy Rock (Book 10)
Thicker Than Water (Book 11)
Redeeming Holy Rock (12)
Whom the Sons Set Free (13)

<u>*Holy Rock Chronicles*</u>
(*"My Son's Wife"* short story spin-off)
SET ONE
(Read after Book 11)
Calling Dr. Daniels (1)
The Woman in Apartment 3D (2)
Ruthless Rianna (3)

<u>*Holy Rock Chronicles set #2*</u>
(*"My Son's Wife"* short story spin-off)
SET TWO
(Read after Book 12)
Christian Black, Esq. (4)
If Your Price is Right (5)
Love Shoulda Brought You Home (6)

Adverse City Series
The Real Housewives of Adverse City 1
The Real Housewives of Adverse City 2
The Real Housewives of Adverse City 3
The Real Housewives of Adverse City 4

Beautiful Ugly 2-book
Beautiful Ugly
True Beauty

Young Adult Titles
House of Cars
The Life of Payne
The Lollipop Girl

Standalone Novels
Always Now and Forever Love Hurts
Into Each Life
Sinsatiable
What's Blood Got To Do With It?
Only In My Dreams
The House Husband
Cross Road
Forever Ain't Enough

Anthologies
Bended Knees
Weary to Will
Learning to Love Me
Show A Little Love I
Show A Little Love II

Nonfiction
A Christian's Perspective: Journey Through
Grief
How to Live Your Life Like It's Golden

Journals
Journal Your Way Through It
Sister Sister Book Log Journal

Contact information
www.sheliaebell.net
www.sheliawritesbooks.com
sheliawritesbooks@yahoo.com
www.facebook.com/sheliawritesbooks
@sheliaebell (Twitter & Instagram)

Join my mailing list
for literary updates and new book release
information
www.sheliawritesbooks.com

If you enjoyed this book or any of my books,
please go to your favorite review site and leave
a positive review!

Other links to my books
bit.ly/sheliaebell
bit.ly/sheliabn
bit.ly/sheliabell

www.sheliawritesbooks.com

#iwriteforfilmandtv
#iwritebestsellers
#iwritepageturners
#iwritenewyorktimesbestsellers
#iamgodsamazinggirl

*Perfect Stories About Imperfect People
Like You...and Me!*